HIP-HOP
hitmakers

THE STORY OF
BAD BOY
ENTERTAINMENT

Jeff Burlingame

MC Mason Crest
Philadelphia

...s ...ty Library
Leabharlann Chontae Laoise
Acc. No. ...13/8882......
Class No. ....J782.42....
Inv. No. .....12701......

Mason Crest
370 Reed Road
Broomall, PA 19008
www.masoncrest.com

Copyright © 2013 by Mason Crest, an imprint of National Highlights, Inc.

All rights reserved. No part of this publication may be reproduced or transmitted in any form or by any means, electronic or mechanical, including photocopying, recording, taping, or any information storage and retrieval system, without permission from the publisher.

Printed and bound in the United States of America.

CPSIA Compliance Information: Batch #HHH040112-2.
For further information, contact Mason Crest at 1-866-MCP-Book

First printing
1 3 5 7 9 8 6 4 2

Library of Congress Cataloging-in-Publication Data

Burlingame, Jeff.
  The story of Bad Boy Entertainment / Jeff Burlingame.
     p. cm. — (Hip-hop hitmakers)
  Includes bibliographical references and index.
  ISBN 978-1-4222-2111-2 (hc)
  ISBN 978-1-4222-2124-2 (pb)
  ISBN 978-1-4222-9463-5 (ebook)
  1. Bad Boy Worldwide Entertainment Group—History. 2. Record labels. I. Title.
  ML3792.B33B87 2012
  338.7'61782421649—dc23
                          2011035325

Photo credits: Associated Press: 32; Getty Images: cover, 23; NY Daily News via Getty Images: 15; Mike Segar/Reuters/Landov: 40; Lions Gate Films/Photofest: 47; used under license from Shutterstock, Inc.: 6, 9; cinemafestival / Shutterstock.com: 38; Featureflash / Shutterstock.com: 26, 35, 37 (top), 51, 55; DFree / Shutterstock.com: 22 (bottom); Adam J. Sablich / Shutterstock.com: 14, 37 (bottom), 45; Derrick Salters / Shutterstock.com: 48 (bottom); Joe Seer / Shutterstock.com: 4, 54; Wikimedia Commons: 10, 41, 48 (top), 53; WireImage: 19, 22 (top), 27, 31.

Contents

Bad Boy Entertainment, established by Sean "Diddy" Combs, has released some of the best-selling albums in hip-hop history.

the dream begins

" *I* was always somebody who closed my eyes and dreamed," Sean Combs once told an interviewer, "but then opened my eyes and saw what I had to do." Big dreams and a single-minded focus on making them a reality would take Combs far. At age 23, inspired by a love of hip-hop, he founded a small rap music label called Bad Boy Entertainment. Through his skills as a record producer, performer, and *entrepreneur*, he built Bad Boy into one of the most successful labels in the industry.

GROWING UP "PUFFY"

Sean John Combs was born November 4, 1969, in Harlem, a mostly African-American neighborhood in the New York City borough of Manhattan. At that time, Harlem was plagued by crime and poverty. But the Combs family lived comfortably—for a while, anyway. Sean's father, Melvin, drove a taxi and had a job with the New York City Board of Education. His mother, Janice, worked as a model.

Melvin Combs died when his son was just three. Sean and his younger sister, Keisha, were always told that their father had been killed in a car accident. For years, Sean accepted the story. But as a young teen, curious about certain details he'd heard regarding his father's activities, Sean went to the public library and looked through some old newspaper clippings. He discovered that his father had actually been murdered. And the killing, evidently, was drug related.

Aerial view of Harlem, the New York neighborhood where Sean Combs lived when he was growing up. In the 1970s, Harlem was known for drugs, crime, and poverty.

Melvin Combs, in addition to holding legitimate jobs, had made money by selling illegal drugs.

After the death of her husband, Janice Combs and her children moved into the apartment of her mother, Jessie Smalls. The future hip-hop *mogul* would credit his grandmother for helping give him a happy childhood. She cared for Sean and Keisha while their mother was at work—which was much of the time. To provide for her family, Janice Combs held several jobs. During the day, she drove a school bus and worked at a daycare center. At night, she took care of children with disabilities.

Yet she somehow found the energy to stay deeply involved in the lives of Keisha and Sean. "My mother, she really held her own," he would tell a reporter in 1998. "She toughened me. I didn't miss a beat not having a father because my mother filled his shoes. She was constantly pushing me. She gave me so much attention and so many different experiences."

Those experiences included getting a taste of life outside of Harlem. When Sean was eight, his mother signed him up for a program run by the Fresh Air Fund, an organization that sponsors summer vacations in rural or suburban areas for poor kids living in New York City. He spent two weeks with an Amish family in Pennsylvania. "I guess that was my mother's idea of a great vacation for me," he recalled, "no electricity, a bunch of farm work, moving horse manure every morning, no telephones so I could contact her." But he loved it, going back summer after summer.

Janice Combs was determined to prevent her son from getting into trouble on the streets. She tried to fill his days with positive activities that taught him important life lessons. She took him to church often. But, in Sean's recollection, the crime and violence in Harlem still made life "very tense . . . it was like a war zone."

In 1972, Janice decided that it would best if she moved her family out of Harlem. They settled in Mount Vernon, a middle-class suburb north of the Bronx borough of New York City.

Sean began delivering newspapers to help his struggling mother pay the bills. He would soon take on a second paper route, as well as a job at an amusement park. "Like a lot of kids who grow up in single-parent homes, I had to get a job much quicker and start thinking about the future much earlier," he recalled.

I used to always get cracked on by the other kids about working at [the amusement park] and having two and three jobs. But I would always say to myself that I wanted to be somebody who makes history, and not selfishly, not for me. I just wanted to make a change. I didn't want to be a person who just lived and died.

When Sean was 14, his mother enrolled him in Mount St. Michael Academy, a private, all-boys Catholic high school in the Bronx. At Mount St. Michael he played football, performed in theater productions, and by all accounts got along well with classmates.

It was during this period that he received the nickname by which millions of people would later know him: Puffy. "It came from a childhood friend," he told *Jet* magazine. "It's a silly reason. Whenever I got mad as a kid, I always used to huff and puff. I had a temper. That's why my friend started calling me Puffy."

=== FAST FACT ===

Puffy was only the first of many nicknames Sean Combs would be given—or would give himself. Others included Puff Daddy, P. Diddy, and Diddy. He also often refers to himself as Sean John, his real first and middle names.

When Sean was young, his family moved to Mount Vernon. The suburb, which borders the Bronx neighborhood of New York, had a population of about 72,000 in the 1970s.

DISCOVERING RAP

Puffy spent a lot of his free time back in Harlem, where he visited his grandmother and friends from his old neighborhood. It was in Harlem that he'd first discovered his passion for hip-hop, which had started among African-American youths in the Bronx, then spread to other sections of New York City. In the new style of music, a rapper spoke or chanted lyrics—often improvised—over the top of musical tracks mixed and manipulated by a DJ. Some of the hip-hop artists Puffy liked early on included Run-D.M.C., LL Cool J, and KRS-One. He also was a big fan of one of the only all-white rap groups of the day, the Beastie Boys.

By his early teens, Puffy had begun hanging out in hip-hop clubs, where he listened to the music and danced. He worked hard to perfect his dance moves. He became good enough to attract the attention of club owners as well as people in the music industry. When still in high school, Puffy was hired to dance in music videos by artists such as the rappers Doug E. Fresh and Babyface and the pop group Fine Young Cannibals.

Howard University was founded in the 1860s, after the Civil War ended. It was meant to provide higher education to African Americans. Some famous graduates include Edward Brooke, who in 1966 became the first African American elected to the U.S. Senate, and Thurgood Marshall, who in 1967 became the first African American appointed to the U.S. Supreme Court.

After graduating from Mount St. Michael's in 1987, Puffy enrolled at Howard University in Washington, D.C. His major was business, and he wasted little time in finding a lucrative business opportunity. Puffy began organizing weekly dance parties. Hundreds of people, sometimes thousands, would attend these parties, which became the talk of Howard's campus. Puffy boosted the attendance—and buzz— by contacting hip-hop artists who were on tour in Washington and inviting them to drop by. Many did.

BIG BREAK

One of the rappers Puffy invited to his parties was a friend from Mount Vernon, Dwight "Heavy D" Myers. In 1987, Myers's group, Heavy D & the Boyz, released their debut album on the Uptown Records label. Based in New York City, Uptown focused on hip-hop and rhythm and blues (R&B) music. Puffy repeatedly begged Heavy D to introduce him to Andre Harrell, the head of Uptown Records.

Puffy had long dreamed of getting a job in the music industry. He'd approached several labels. He'd even interviewed for an internship with Def Jam Recordings, a groundbreaking label that produced

RAP AND HIP-HOP

Most music historians date the beginning of commercial rap music to 1979. In August of that year, a group called the Sugarhill Gang released "Rapper's Delight." The first hip-hop single to go gold, it helped introduce rap to a mainstream audience.

A few weeks before "Rapper's Delight" appeared, the Fatback Band released "King Tim III (Personality Jock)." This may be the first commercially released hip-hop single, but it never achieved the popularity of "Rapper's Delight."

Rap had existed before either song, however. It had simply not yet crossed over into the mainstream. Rap, or street poetry, was born out of a cultural movement that started on the streets of New York City in the early 1970s. Rapping was just one element of the developing artistic culture. Other elements included different types of dancing, including break dancing; certain types of urban dress; and graffiti. The culture eventually became known as hip-hop. Today, rap music continues to evolve. It has incorporated other styles of music into its mixes, including rock and roll, soul, and jazz.

FAST FACT

Def Jam Recordings had established itself as a favorite among young listeners by the time Puffy interviewed for an internship there in 1990. Cofounded by Rick Rubin and Russell Simmons, Def Jam had released albums by several of Puffy's favorite rappers, including LL Cool J and the Beastie Boys.

some of hip-hop's biggest acts. Nothing had panned out, however.

Eventually, Heavy D came through for his friend, arranging for Puffy to meet Andre Harrell. The Uptown Records president was impressed by the eager college student. Harrell offered Puffy an unpaid internship. Puffy accepted.

It was hardly a glamorous position. Puffy would be expected to run errands and perform any other tasks Uptown staff asked him to do. In addition, traveling between Washington, D.C., and Uptown's offices in New York City required a four-hour train ride—each way. Yet Puffy was thrilled by the chance to get a start in the music industry.

He was determined to make the most of the opportunity. Puffy did everything asked of him with enthusiasm and attention to detail. When he talked with experienced Uptown staffers, he frequently took notes, which he would later study. He wanted to learn everything he could about the music industry.

Harrell, who later called Puffy the "hardest working intern ever," became his *mentor*. He gave Puffy increasing responsibilities.

At the beginning of his internship, Puffy went to New York a couple times each week. He'd leave Washington after his college classes were done for the day and make the return trip late at night, so he could attend classes the next day. But as his responsibilities at Uptown grew, so did the amount of time he had to spend at the label's New York offices. The schedule soon became too much for Puffy to handle. He had to choose between school and work. In 1990, he dropped out of Howard. "I was serious about my studies in the beginning," Puffy recalled, "but my mind was moving too fast for it. My dreams were bigger."

At the invitation of his mentor, Puffy moved into Harrell's mansion in New Jersey. Uptown Records had signed a deal with industry giant MCA Records, and Harrell was living large off the money from that deal. Puffy wanted that kind of lifestyle for himself.

Around this time, while working on a script for a proposed film about an Uptown artist, screenwriter Barry Michael Cooper met Puffy. "When you write your next movie, keep me in mind," Cooper says the young man told him. "My name is Sean, but they call me Puffy. And I'm gonna be a big star."

It would be a while before he'd be classified as a "star," but Puffy quickly rose through Uptown's ranks. Within a year, he was promoted to vice president of talent and marketing. One of the first acts he worked with was Jodeci, a young R&B group. Jodeci had a wholesome feel, but Puffy worked to give the group a harder edge. It paid off: Jodeci's first studio album, 1991's *Forever My Lady*, hit number one on the R&B charts and spawned three hit singles.

Puffy also produced the debut album of Mary J. Blige, *What's the 411?* It reached number six on the Billboard 200 pop albums chart.

Puffy's successes won him another promotion, this time to vice president of Uptown Records. He was only 22 years old. His career as a music industry mogul appeared well on its way.

TRAGEDY

Although he now had a good job in the music industry—and the

Puffy produced Mary J. Blige's first album, What's the 411?, *for Uptown Records. It established the young singer as a major R&B star.*

fancy cars and clothes that went along with it—not everything was rosy in Puffy's world. In addition to his job at Uptown, he had continued promoting his own events—and one of them would turn tragic. In December 1991, Puffy had organized a basketball game and concert at the City College of New York (CCNY). The event was supposed to help raise money for an AIDS charity. However, too many tickets were sold, and security was terribly inadequate. Shortly before the event was to begin, the large crowd surged forward through the lone entrance to the gym. Nine people suffocated or were crushed to death.

The incident also brought Puffy a great deal of negative publicity. Criminal charges against him seemed possible, but no such charges were ever filed. Still, a court would eventually order Puffy to pay $750,000 to the victims' families as part of a settlement.

After taking some time off to focus on his legal affairs, Puffy returned to work at Uptown. He continued his successful ways there. His dress grew flashier, and he gathered an *entourage*. He began taking steps to start his own record label, which he would call Bad Boy Entertainment.

For a time, Harrell helped his *protégé* with this undertaking. But

RACING × × × FINAL

STOLEN ICON RETURNED

Holy Image back in St. Irene's – Page 7

DAILY ◉ NEWS

FORWARD WITH NEW YORK

1.00

Sunday, December 29, 1991

HORROR

Woman is wheeled from the City College gym as hundreds of rap music fans stampeded after being shut out of a celebrity basketball game.

MARCEL HYACINTHE

8 CRUSHED TO DEATH AT CCNY RAP BENEFIT

PAGES 2-3

A New York newspaper reports on the fatal concert that Puffy had promoted in December 1991. Eight people died that night; a ninth person succumbed to injuries a few days later. Puffy was blamed for selling more than 5,000 tickets when the arena only seated 2,700 people. A shortage of security guards contributed to the problem. Puffy was devastated by the CCNY tragedy. "I started to lose it," he later said. "I felt like I didn't even want to live no more."

Puffy soon fell out of favor with his mentor. Various explanations for the rift have been given. Several sources at Uptown Records say that Puffy had become impossibly *egotistical* and could not be managed.

Whatever the reason, Harrell fired Puffy in 1993. Puffy took the news hard. "I cried for a coupl'a days and felt like I wanted to jump off a building," he recalled. "I felt like I didn't know everything to be able to make educated decisions."

The firing—along with the CCNY tragedy—could easily have brought an end to Puffy's dreams of stardom. But he refused to give up. He was determined to make Bad Boy a success. At the outset, however, Bad Boy was anything but a big player. Strapped for cash, Puffy had to run his label from his mother's house.

bad boy is born

After being fired from Uptown Records, Sean Combs threw his energies into establishing his own Bad Boy label. Fortunately, he was able to take a promising new artist with him to Bad Boy. That artist's name was Christopher Wallace.

In early 1992, Puffy had been given Wallace's demo tape by an acquaintance at the hip-hop magazine *The Source.* "As soon as I put it on, it just bugged me out," Puffy recalled of the demo. "I couldn't stop listening to it. I listened to it for days and days, hours and hours. And his voice just hypnotized me."

Puffy's acquaintance at *The Source* knew Wallace was from Brooklyn, but he didn't have an address or phone number for the rapper. Puffy set about tracking Wallace down. His sleuthing led to an overweight 19-

Christoper "Notorious B.I.G." Wallace soon became the biggest star signed to Bad Boy Records.

year-old who had a criminal record for weapons and drug charges and who had built an underground following as a rapper named Quest. Puffy quickly signed Wallace to a contract with Uptown Records.

Wallace made several guest appearances on songs by other Uptown artists. But before he could complete his own album, Andre Harrell fired Puffy Combs. Wallace decided to sign with Puffy's Bad Boy label.

Puffy had already been working to give the young rapper's image a makeover. He'd convinced Wallace to drop the stage name Quest in favor of "Biggie Smalls." Next, Puffy set about honing Wallace's style. He believed Wallace could achieve big success as a gangsta rapper.

Rap had developed in New York City, and for several years the hip-hop *genre* was dominated by East Coast artists and record labels. In the early years, much of the music dealt with fun themes, such as parties, dancing, and the skills of the rapper—though some songs criticized racism and other injustices in American society.

Beginning in the late 1980s, however, a new style of hip-hop music began to gain popularity. Called gangsta rap, it was much harder edged. It painted a grim picture of life in America's inner cities. Its songs—which often contained very *explicit* lyrics—depicted rampant drug abuse, violence, and mistreatment of women. Yet the songs didn't criticize this behavior. On the contrary, they frequently seemed to glorify the gangster lifestyle.

While gangsta rap was very controversial, by the early 1990s it was also very popular. It was, in fact, the most commercially successful form of hip-hop music. Artists from the West Coast—including Ice-T, N.W.A., Dr. Dre, and Snoop Doggy Dogg—led the way. Their popularity fueled profits for West Coast labels, especially Los Angeles–based Death Row Records.

A B.I.G. HIT

Puffy Combs believed that in Biggie Smalls he'd found someone who could compete with the most hard-core of the West Coast gangsta rappers. Biggie knew firsthand what it was like to survive on violence-filled streets, to sell drugs, and to spend time behind bars. And he was able to rap about his experiences in a vivid way.

On September 13, 1994, Bad Boy released *Ready to Die*. It was the debut album of the Notorious B.I.G., the stage name Christopher Wallace adopted after he and Puffy discovered that another rapper was already using the name Biggie Smalls. *Ready to Die* was also the first album on the Bad Boy label, and Puffy could hardly have hoped for a better beginning. Critics and fans alike loved Biggie's smooth delivery, deep-toned voice, and blunt, honest lyrics. The Notorious B.I.G., *Rolling Stone* magazine writer Cheo Coker raved, "sweeps his verbal camera high and low, painting a sonic picture so vibrant that you're transported right to the scene. He raps in clear, sparse terms, allowing the lyrics to hit the first time you hear them."

> **FAST FACT**
>
> Like Sean Combs, his mentor, Christopher Wallace had more than his share of nicknames. In addition to Biggie and the Notorious B.I.G., Wallace was known as Big Poppa and Frank White.

The 17 tracks drew heavily on Biggie's own experiences as a drug dealer and petty criminal, though clearly not everything on the album was meant to be taken as autobiographical. On the final track, "Suicidal Thoughts," Biggie takes a stark look at a misspent life. He raps:

All my life I been considered as the worst
Lyin' to my mother, even stealin' out her purse. . . .
Forgive me for my disrespect, forgive me for my lies

At the end of the song, weary and depressed, he commits suicide.

Ready to Die reached number 14 on the Billboard 200 albums chart. It eventually sold 4 million copies. Two singles, "Big Poppa" and "One More Chance," also reached **platinum** status (meaning they each sold more than a million copies).

MORE SUCCESSES

Just a week after *Ready to Die* hit record stores, Bad Boy's second album was released. *Project: Funk da World* was the solo debut of rapper Craig Mack. Sales—though not as spectacular as those of the Notorious B.I.G.'s first outing—were solid. *Project: Funk da World* went **gold**, and one of its singles, "Flava in Ya Ear," was a platinum seller.

> **═══FAST FACT═══**
>
> Established in 1894, *Billboard* is a weekly magazine dedicated to the music industry. For more than three-quarters of a century, its music charts have become the standard by which musicians in most genres of music measure their success.

The success of *Ready to Die* and *Project: Funk da World* helped establish Bad Boy Records as a serious player in the music industry. So, too, did a lucrative distribution deal Puffy had secured with Arista Records. All of this enabled Puffy to expand his label in important ways. First, he moved Bad Boy's operations out of his mother's house and into new offices in New York. Second, he began signing new artists. They included R&B singer Faith Evans (who had married Biggie shortly before the release of his first album), rapper Mase, and the R&B groups 112 and Total. All of these acts would notch platinum albums for Bad Boy.

Puffy's talents as a producer were also in great demand, thanks largely to his production work on *Ready to Die*. He was hired to work with acts such as Babyface, Mariah Carey, and New Edition.

Artists like the rapper Mase (left, with Puffy at an awards show) and singer Faith Evans (below) helped Bad Boy become successful.

Puffy Combs, still in his mid-20s, appeared to be living a charmed life. Only a few years after he'd founded Bad Boy, the label was fast becoming one of the music industry's major players. Whatever Puffy touched, it seemed, turned to gold—if not platinum. But Puffy and Bad Boy were headed for some difficult and deadly times.

EAST COAST VS. WEST COAST

On the night of November 30, 1994, the rapper Tupac Shakur and several friends went to New York City's Quad Recording Studios. There, Shakur was supposed to make a guest appearance on a CD being produced by an acquaintance. He never got the chance. Gunmen were waiting in the lobby of the recording studio. They shot Shakur five times and took $40,000 worth of jewelry from him. One of the rapper's friends was also shot.

Shakur and his friends jumped in an elevator and rode upstairs to the studio. Among the people gathered there were Puffy Combs and Biggie Smalls, a close friend of Shakur's. Shakur, who survived the shooting, would come to believe that Biggie and Puffy had set him up to be murdered. It was a charge they strongly denied. But the incident helped set the stage for a bitter feud that would soon engulf Puffy, Bad Boy, and much of the hip-hop community.

On August 3, 1995, Marion "Suge" Knight lit the fuse of what would become known as the East Coast–West Coast hip-hop war. The venue was New York City's Paramount Theater, where the biggest stars in rap music had gathered for the second annual Source Hip-Hop Music Awards show. Knight, the head of Death Row Records, took the stage to present an award. Instead of merely congratulating the recipient, he used the opportunity to mock a rival. "If you don't want the owner of your label on your album or in your video or on your tour," Knight said to the crowd, "come sign with Death Row."

Insulting comments by Death Row Records president Suge Knight (right) started the East Coast–West Coast hip-hop feud.

DEATH ROW RECORDS

At the time its feud with Bad Boy Entertainment began, Death Row Records was arguably the most powerful and influential label in hip-hop music. Death Row was founded in 1991 by Marion "Suge" Knight and Andre "Dr. Dre" Young. Knight, a former college football star, handled business and marketing matters at the label. Dr. Dre, a rapper and music producer, was in charge of Death Row's creative direction. Formerly a member of the pioneering gangsta rap group N.W.A., Dre developed a distinctive musical style known as G-funk. It helped hard-core gangsta rap achieve **crossover** appeal.

Death Row's first release, Dre's own *The Chronic* (1992), was a huge critical and commercial success. It ultimately sold more than 3 million copies. The label's next album, *Doggystyle* (1993), was even bigger. The solo debut of 22-year-old Cordazar Calvin Broadus—better known as Snoop Doggy Dogg—it became the first hip-hop release ever to enter the Billboard 200 albums chart at number one. *Doggystyle* went on to sell 4 million copies.

Six straight Death Row releases reached number one on the Billboard 200 albums chart between 1994 and 1996: the soundtrack *Murder Was the Case; Tha Dogg Pound's Dogg Food; All Eyez on Me* and *The Don Kiluminati: The 7 Day Theory*, both from Tupac Shakur; Snoop Doggy Dogg's *Tha Doggfather*; and *Gridlock'd*, another soundtrack.

Suge Knight once explained that the reason he'd chosen the name Death Row was that nearly everybody associated with the label had gotten into trouble with the law. That applied to Knight himself. Over the years, he'd been charged with crimes ranging from attempted murder and assault with a deadly weapon to auto theft. Yet he'd always managed to avoid a prison sentence. That changed after the September 1996 assault of Crips gang member Orlando Anderson in Las Vegas. Knight's participation in the beating violated the terms of his probation from an earlier assault case, and in 1997 a judge sentenced him to nine years in prison. With its president behind bars, Death Row Records went into a tailspin from which it never recovered.

As just about everyone understood, Puffy Combs was the label owner to whom Knight was referring. Puffy had a reputation for rapping on his artists' albums, appearing in their videos, and, in general, enjoying the spotlight. The audience at the Source Hip-Hop Music Awards didn't seem to know quite how to react to Knight's comments. A few screamed at the Death Row president. Others cheered. Many would interpret Knight's words as an insult not only to Puffy Combs but also to Bad Boy's artists and East Coast rappers in general.

Puffy tried to defuse the tension. Later in the evening, when it was his turn to present an award, Puffy spoke about the need for "unity" in the hip-hop world. He also hugged the recipient of the award he was presenting, Death Row artist Snoop Doggy Dogg. The damage, however, had been done. The East Coast–West Coast feud was under way.

Blood would soon be shed. On September 24, 1995, Puffy and Biggie attended a birthday party for rap producer Jermaine Dupri at the Atlanta nightclub Platinum House. Suge Knight and his entourage were also in attendance. A fight broke out, and Jake Robles, a close friend of Knight's, was shot. He died a week later.

Police were unable to identify the shooter, and no one was ever prosecuted for the crime. However, some witnesses pointed the finger at one of Puffy's bodyguards.

Knight believed Puffy had something to do with the murder of his friend. Puffy insisted that wasn't the case. In an attempt to end the feud, Puffy sent the son of a famous African-American minister to Los Angeles to talk with Knight. But the Death Row head refused even to meet with Puffy's representative. An associate of Knight's told a reporter that Knight would "settle the beef his way. On the street."

Suge Knight believed that Puffy was responsible for the death of his friend at a party for music producer Jermaine Dupri (pictured).

That wasn't a claim to be taken lightly. Knight had a well-earned reputation for violent behavior. He was also widely rumored to have deep connections with the Bloods, a notorious street gang. Puffy Combs soon hired bodyguards for his protection. So did Biggie Smalls. Some of these bodyguards were rumored to be members of the Crips, a street gang that was the sworn enemy of the Bloods.

THE KILLING OF TUPAC

Just three weeks after the murder of Jake Robles, Knight took another step that would only add to the hostility between East Coast and West Coast rappers, and between the Bad Boy and Death Row labels. Knight posted bail for Tupac Shakur —who'd been in prison while his 1994 conviction on assault charges was being appealed—and signed the rapper to a recording contract with Death Row.

Shakur soon joined the East Coast–West Coast war. In the lyrics to some of his songs, he expressed contempt for Puffy Combs and

Death Row Records stars Snoop Dogg (left) and Tupac Shakur (right) contributed to the East Coast–West Coast feud by recording songs that dissed Bad Boy, Puffy, and Biggie. Three days after this photo was taken, Tupac was shot in Las Vegas.

Biggie Smalls, who he thought had dissed him in Biggie's 1995 single "Who Shot Ya?" Bad Boy artists fired back by recording their own verbal jabs directed at Death Row artists.

The diss tracks turned into a real-life scuffle on March 29, 1996. Shakur and Biggie were both backstage at the Soul Train Music Awards in Los Angeles when a fight broke out. Biggie's bodyguard pulled a gun, as did a member of Shakur's entourage. But no shots were fired.

About two months later, in early June, Death Row Records released Shakur's single "Hit 'em Up." In it he called out, in particularly ugly terms, Biggie Smalls, also dissing Puffy, Bad Boy, and various East Coast rappers. "We're gonna kill all you," he promised.

On September 7, 1996, Shakur was in Las Vegas, Nevada, along with Suge Knight and members of the Death Row entourage. As they were leaving the casino where they had watched a heavyweight boxing match, Shakur spotted a young man named Orlando Anderson. A member of the Crips, Anderson had apparently participated in an earlier beating of one of Shakur's bodyguards. This time he was on the receiving end as Shakur, Knight, and several Death Row bodyguards pummeled and stomped him.

A couple hours later, Shakur was hit by four bullets in a drive-by shooting. He died six days later.

Las Vegas police questioned Orlando Anderson in connection with the killing, but he was never charged. The case remains unsolved.

Because no one was ever arrested for the murder, theories about who killed Tupac Shakur—and why—abounded. Many people immediately speculated that the rapper was a victim of the East Coast–West Coast rap war—and specifically, that Bad Boy was to blame. One newspaper published a story saying that Biggie Smalls had arranged his former friend's killing. Biggie denied this, and much of the information on which the story was based turned out to be false.

Even in the absence of proof, suspicions that Bad Boy had been involved in Shakur's murder put Puffy and his associates in danger. "We was shocked at first," Puffy said of the killing. "And we was hurt. It was like, '. . .why'd that have to happen?' Then we became scared, because we know how the media is. The news reports in the early couple of days, all in L.A. and Las Vegas, had our pictures. We were the ones they were pointing their fingers to."

THE MUSIC MUST GO ON

Scared or not, Puffy forged on with his business of producing successful hip-hop records. Most notably, there was the follow-up album to Biggie's successful debut. The new record, a double album, was to be called *Life After Death*. Its 24 tracks included **collaborations** with other talented artists, including Lil' Kim, R. Kelly, Mase, Jay-Z, and, of course, Puffy.

Released on March 25, 1997, *Life After Death* soon rocketed to the top of the Billboard 200 albums chart. Two singles from the album, "Hypnotize" and "Mo Money Mo Problems," also reached number one on the charts.

Like Biggie's debut album, *Life After Death* was well received by the critics. Writing in the *Los Angeles Times*, Cheo Coker noted:

> *In key moments, B.I.G. does a marvelous job of surfing between accessible music fare tailored for the radio ("Mo Money Mo Problems") and more challenging material ("Kick In The Door") that will be savored by hard-core rap fans who have long admired B.I.G.'s microphone skills. Rarely has a rapper attempted to please so many different audiences—and done it so brilliantly.*

The *Life After Death* album cover featured Biggie standing next to a black hearse (a limousine for carrying coffins to the cemetery). On its license plate were the initials "B.I.G." The image was both unsettling and heartrending. That's because, at the time of the album's release, the rapper had been dead for two weeks.

Biggie had gone to Los Angeles for the Soul Train Music Awards, the same gathering where an altercation between West Coast and East Coast rappers had broken out the year before. For the 1997 show, held on March 8, Biggie helped present an award. As he stepped up to the microphone to announce the winner, many in the crowd booed loudly. Biggie was, after all, on the West Coast rappers' turf, and they let him know it.

After the show, Biggie and other members of the Bad Boy crew attended a party held at the Petersen Auto Museum. Shortly after midnight on March 9, the party dispersed. Biggie left in an SUV. He was riding in the front passenger seat. Not far from the museum, as the SUV was stopped at a red light, a black car pulled up alongside it. The driver of that car pointed a handgun at Biggie and began firing. Biggie, hit four times, was rushed to the hospital, where he died less than an hour later. Christopher "Biggie" Wallace was just 24 years old.

Many people assumed that Biggie had been killed in retaliation for the murder of Tupac Shakur, his rival and former friend. Suge Knight, in prison at the time, was widely rumored to have ordered Biggie's murder. A statement issued by Death Row denied any involvement on the

> **FAST FACT**
>
> In 2000, the Notorious B.I.G. album *Life After Death* achieved diamond status, meaning it had sold 10 million copies.

Biggie and Puffy attend the Soul Train Music Awards in Los Angeles, March 8, 1997. Early the next morning, Biggie was murdered in a drive-by shooting.

Fans of the Notorious B.I.G. watch as his funeral procession passes through the streets of the Brooklyn neighborhood where he once lived, March 1997.

part of Knight or the label. "It's ludicrous for anyone out there to blame Death Row," the statement read. "We do not condone this type of activity . . . Death Row knows how bad something like this can feel. It happened in our backyard with Tupac just a few months ago." Like the slaying of Shakur, the murder of Biggie remains unsolved.

At the time of the shooting, Puffy Combs was riding in a car directly in front of Biggie's SUV. When he heard the shots, Puffy rushed back to the SUV in a futile attempt to help his friend. In the aftermath of Biggie's death, Puffy was numb. "I just could not move," he recalled about eight months later.

> *I was stuck. I just did not want to leave him. . . . I didn't really want to accept it. So then I'm about to get on a plane. And as I'm seeing the plane pull up, that's when I just break down. I'm about to leave L.A. without my man, you know what I'm saying? He's getting left here—he's at the morgue, just laying there. . . . I just wanted him to be with me, sitting right there with me, going back to New York. I would just sleep a lot. I just wanted to wake up. I just knew it was a dream.*

Of course, Biggie's death had not been a dream. It was as real as could be, and it would have an enormous impact on Puffy and Bad Boy for years to come.

3

Puffy hits the stage

Puffy had long been involved in the performance end of the music business. As a teen, he'd danced in clubs and in videos. As an adult, he'd rapped on the albums and danced in the videos of Bad Boy artists. But Biggie's death pushed Puffy further into the spotlight. In tribute to his late friend, Puffy—under the stage name Puff Daddy—recorded a song called "I'll Be Missing You." Over samples of "Every Breath You Take," a 1983 hit song by the Police, Puffy rapped about how he missed Biggie, the good times they'd had together, and how he believed the two would meet again one day. The song's chorus was sung by Biggie's widow, Faith Evans. The Bad Boy group 112 also performed on "I'll Be Missing You."

PUFF DADDY, RECORDING STAR

"I'll Be Missing You," released in May 1997, was a major commercial success. The song topped the Billboard Hot 100 singles chart for 11 weeks and became the best-selling song Bad Boy had ever released.

"I'll Be Missing You" helped carry Puffy's debut album, *No Way Out*, to the top of the Billboard 200 albums chart. Other hits on the album included "Can't Nobody Hold Me Down" (also a number-one single), "It's All About the Benjamins," and "Been Around the World." *No Way Out* was eventually certified 7x platinum.

Sales notwithstanding, some critics weren't especially fond of *No Way Out*. A few said Puffy's songs were unoriginal and used too many samples from other artists' material. Yet many critics gave Puffy's work the thumbs up. For example, Leo Stanley of the music Web site *All Music Guide* wrote that *No Way Out* was "a compelling, harrowing album that establishes Puff Daddy as a vital rapper in his own right."

Puffy was also honored by his peers in the recording industry. *No Way Out* won the Grammy Award for Best Rap Album, and "I'll Be Missing You" took the Grammy for Best Rap Performance by a Duo or Group.

Almost overnight, it seemed, Puffy had gone from successful

With the 1997 album No Way Out, *Puffy showed that he could succeed as a rap performer. Here, he accepts a Billboard Music Award in December 1997.*

record executive to superstar performer. At the MTV Video Music Awards, he sang and danced to "I'll Be Missing You," with the Police's Sting, Faith Evans, and 112 singing the choruses as Biggie's videos played on a large monitor in the background.

By 1997 Bad Boy's biggest rival, Death Row Records, was in disarray. Its president, Suge Knight, was in prison, and many of the label's stars moved on. With the decline of Death Row, the East Coast–West Coast feud also faded. Bad Boy's star, meanwhile, shone brighter than ever. So did that of the label's head. Many top artists sought out Puffy, who appeared to have the golden touch. Even Puffy's venture into rock and roll with a guitar-led remake of "It's All About the Benjamins," featuring Foo Fighter frontman Dave Grohl, became a hit. In a short time, Puffy had become hip-hop's biggest star. He'd also become its richest. In 1997 alone, Puffy earned $200 million.

Puffy's second solo album, *Forever*, was released in August 1999. Behind the hit single "Satisfy You," Forever debuted as the number two album in the country. Though the album was certified platinum, it didn't come close to matching the commercial or critical success of *No Way Out*. Many peo-

> **FAST FACT**
>
> Puff Daddy's musical tribute to Biggie Smalls, "I'll Be Missing You," outsold every other single in 1997 except "Candle in the Wind" by Elton John. When originally released in 1974, the song had been about actress Marilyn Monroe. The 1997 version honored the memory of Britain's Princess Diana, who died in a car crash on August 31 of that year.

> **FAST FACT**
>
> When he played on Puffy's "All About the Benjamins," Dave Grohl was the singer and guitarist for the rock band Foo Fighters. But Grohl first became famous in a different musical role. From 1990 to 1994, he was the drummer for the legendary rock group Nirvana.

ple suggested that stardom had gone to Puffy's head, and that his skills as a rapper weren't nearly as great as he imagined. "His sophomoric, monotone raps," wrote Soren Baker of the *Los Angeles Times*, "drain the fire and passion from some otherwise noteworthy collaborations with Jay-Z, Twista, Lil' Kim and others. . . . Puff Daddy is much more tolerable as a second fiddle who adds an occasional rap, as he did in the past on albums from far more capable protégés such as the Notorious B.I.G. and Mase."

On his second album, Puffy teamed up with rap stars like Lil' Kim (right) and Jay-Z (below).

Puffy dated the popular actress and singer Jennifer Lopez for more than two years.

CONTROVERSIES

Despite the lukewarm response to his second album, Puffy remained a huge celebrity. It seemed that every move he made became a news story somewhere. Puffy certainly made effective use of his celebrity to promote his label—and himself. But he also discovered the downside of celebrity.

On the night of December 27, 1999, Puffy was in a Manhattan nightclub called Club New York with friends and members of his entourage. They included Puffy's girlfriend, actress and singer

Jennifer Lopez; up-and-coming rapper Jamal "Shyne" Barrow; and Anthony "Wolf" Jones, one of Puffy's bodyguards. Around 3 a.m., Puffy and Barrow got into a dispute with another group of people at the club. A fight broke out, and in the melee handguns were fired. Three bystanders were wounded.

Police apprehended Barrow at Club New York. But Puffy, along with Lopez and Jones, fled the scene in an SUV driven by a chauffeur. The SUV was later stopped, and when police searched the vehicle, they found an unregistered handgun.

Puffy and Jones were eventually charged with criminal possession of a firearm. They were also charged with attempting to bribe a wit-

JAMAL "SHYNE" BARROW

Before his involvement in the Club New York shooting, Jamal "Shyne" Barrow seemed to have a bright future as a rapper. Born in Belize in 1978, Shyne was seven when he and his single mother moved to Brooklyn. There he became involved in crime. At 15, Shyne was shot in the shoulder.

After that incident, Shyne started to turn his life around. He was discovered rapping in a barbershop and soon was introduced to Puffy Combs. Puffy liked Shyne's deep voice, which was similar to that of Biggie Smalls, and signed him to Bad Boy Records.

Shyne was working on his debut album when the Club New York shooting occurred. Released in 2000, the self-titled *Shyne* sold relatively well. The next year, however, the rapper was sent to prison. His second album, *Godfather Buried Alive*, was released in 2004, while he was still behind bars. It sold about half as many copies as his first album had.

Shyne served eight years before being released in 2009. Because he was not a citizen of the United States, U.S. laws required that Shyne be deported back to his home country.

ness, for allegedly offering the chauffeur $50,000 to say the gun found in the SUV belonged to him. Among the charges Shyne faced were attempted murder, assault, and *reckless endangerment*.

The trial, which began in January 2001, became a media circus. Puffy was painted in starkly different terms. Some reports characterized him as a hard-working entrepreneur who'd gotten caught up in an unfortunate situation. Other reports noted that Puffy seemed to have adopted the thuggish posture represented by gangsta rap. Those who saw Puffy as a would-be gangster cited another incident, from April 1999. On that occasion, Puffy and two associates from Bad Boy had allegedly beaten Steve Stoute, an executive from the rival

Some of Puffy's fans hold signs showing their support outside the Manhattan courthouse where his trial was held in 2001.

View of the entrance to the Bad Boy Entertainment office in downtown New York.

Interscope Records label. Puffy had appeared in a music video for one of Stoute's clients, rapper Nas. Afterward, Puffy had asked that a controversial scene from the video be cut, which Stoute had declined to do. So Puffy and his associates had gone to Stoute's office and roughed him up. Ultimately Puffy pleaded guilty to a minor charge and was sentenced to one day of anger-management treatment.

In March 2001, after a two-month trial, Puffy was found not guilty of all the charges he faced in the Club New York shooting. Anthony Jones was also acquitted on all charges. But Barrow was found guilty of assault and reckless endangerment, and he was sentenced to 10 years in prison. Puffy, who'd been grooming Barrow as his protégé, called the sentence "unfair and extreme," and added, "I know he had no intention of hurting anyone. . . . I'm shocked by [the] outcome."

Despite his acquittal, all the negative publicity surrounding the trial took a toll on Puffy's popularity. Some people considered him a punk. Others suggested he was washed up at age 30. That was a claim

found in multiple newspaper and magazine articles. One such article
ran in the *Washington Post* under the headline "The Deflation of Puffy
Combs: He Powered a Hip-Hop Empire and Made a Lot of Enemies.
Some Are Relishing His Loss of Steam." The story, written by Lonnae
O'Neal Parker, began:

> *Some folks are saying Sean "Puffy" Combs is played. Done.
> Over, at 30. That his jiggy, which helped define this half-
> decade in popular culture, is up. When he was spotted in
> Harlem's Apollo Theatre at a performance of the heavy
> metal band Korn a couple of weeks ago, some audience
> members began chanting "Puffy sucks." ... He's even e-hated
> in anti-Puffy Web sites, with one featuring a graphic of him
> being shot, supposedly for exploiting the death of his label's
> star Christopher Wallace, aka the Notorious B.I.G.*

Another article, this one by Jeannine Amber in *Vibe* magazine, put
it this way. "Rub your followers the wrong way—with a mediocre
album and a cocky attitude—and they'll knock you off your pedestal
in a hot second."

By 2001, it appeared that Puffy had been knocked down. Would he
be able to get back on his feet? That was the million-dollar question.

tough times

Between 1999 and March 2001, as Puffy Combs's image was tarnished by negative publicity and legal troubles, Bad Boy continued to churn out modestly successful records. Over that span, the label released eight albums that would eventually be certified platinum. They included *Double Up* by Mase; *Forever* by Puff Daddy; *Life Story*, the debut of rapper Black Rob; *Emotional*, the debut of R&B singer Carl Thomas; Shyne's self-titled debut; *It Was All a Dream*, from the girl group Dream; and *Part III* by 112.

But by far the most popular Bad Boy album from this period was *Born Again*, the second **posthumous** album from the Notorious B.I.G. Released in December 1999, *Born Again* quickly shot to the top of the Billboard 200 chart. Although the raps were leftover rhymes that

Biggie had recorded for previous albums, *Born Again* included an all-star crew of guests. They included Snoop Dogg, Eminem, Ice Cube, Missy Elliott, Busta Rhymes, and, of course, Puffy. The critical reception to *Born Again* was generally positive, though some writers—as well as some fans—wondered whether Puffy was exploiting the memory of his dead friend.

TROUBLES IN THE BAD BOY FAMILY

Not all of Puffy's artists were happy with their situations at Bad Boy. In 1999, Mase decided to give up his career in rap music and become a minister. Around the same time, the hip-hop group the Lox began

THE STORY OF MASE

Mason "Mase" Betha was born in Jacksonville, Florida, in 1977. At age five, he moved to Harlem with his family. But after he became involved with the wrong crowd, his mother sent him back to Florida to live. Two years later, he returned to New York, where he graduated from high school. He won a basketball scholarship to the State University of New York at Purchase but dropped out after completing just one year to pursue a career in hip-hop.

At a party in Atlanta hosted by the producer Jermaine Dupri, Mase met Puffy Combs, who immediately signed him to a contract with Bad Boy. Mase's first album, *Harlem World*, was released in late 1997. It rocketed to number one on the Billboard 200 chart and eventually sold more than 4 million copies. Mase's second album, *Double Up* (1999), went platinum as well.

Mase discovered religion and, following the release of *Double Up*, retired from the music industry. He worked with inner-city youth, wrote a book, and became a motivational speaker.

He returned to the music industry in 2004, releasing his third album, *Welcome Back*, on the Bad Boy label.

Jadakiss and the other members of rap group The Lox decided to leave Bad Boy. They felt the label did not have the right image.

waging a highly publicized and bitter campaign to be released from their contract with Bad Boy. Lox members wanted to shed the glossy image and watered-down music they'd become known for with Puffy's label in favor of hard-core rap.

Faith Evans, too, had become dissatisfied with Bad Boy. Evans had creative differences with Puffy for some time, but tensions came to a head in 2001. The singer believed that Puffy had become too focused on his own career and wasn't putting enough time into promoting hers. In particular, she didn't think that Bad Boy had made enough effort to promote her album *Faithfully*. Evans decided it was time to ask Puffy to release her from her contract so she could sign with another record label. "Working with someone like Puff is like being in a marriage," Evans wrote in her 2008 book, *Keep the Faith*. "And sometimes, when you realize the love is just not what it used to be, it may be hard for you to let go and move on. Even if you know it's the right thing to do."

NEW LEASE ON LIFE

For his part, Puffy had decided he needed something of a clean start as well. After his March 2001 acquittal—and after having broken up with Jennifer Lopez, his girlfriend of two years—he gave himself a new name. The man who had gone from Sean Combs to Puffy to Puff Daddy was now to be known as "P. Diddy."

In July 2001, *The Saga Continues*, a new album from P. Diddy & the Bad Boy Family, was released. It debuted at number two on the Billboard 200 chart. The album's singles included the semi-autobiographical songs "Diddy" and "Bad Boy for Life," which claimed that the Bad Boy label was back on top. In truth, Bad Boy was nowhere near as successful as it once had been. But *The Saga Continues* did sell well, eventually going platinum. Critics gave the album mixed reviews. "The man formerly known as Puff Daddy has released a thoroughly satisfying album," wrote Soren Baker in the *Los Angeles Times*. "That is not a misprint. . . . P. Diddy rockets back to respectability." On the other hand, *Entertainment Weekly* magazine only gave the album an average rating.

The Saga Continues was released the same year P. Diddy publicly announced plans to take a break from the entertainment industry. But ultimately he took very little—if any—time off. Instead, he merely shifted his focus from music to other endeavors for a short period.

He began acting, appearing in the critically acclaimed movie *Monster's Ball*. He also searched for new musical talent on the MTV reality TV show *Making the Band 2*.

The period 2002–2004 wasn't exactly a golden age for Bad Boy. The label did notch two platinum-selling albums. One, a 2002 compilation of remixed

=== FAST FACT ===

The winner of *Making the Band 2* was a six-member group that eventually wound up calling itself Da Band. The group released one album on the Bad Boy label, 2003's *Too Hot for T.V.*, before breaking up.

songs from Bad Boy artists called *We Invented the Remix: Volume 1*, sold 2 million copies. The other, released the following year, was the soundtrack to the coincidentally titled film *Bad Boys II*. The album—featuring songs from stars such as Jay-Z, Beyonce, the Notorious B.I.G., Snoop Dogg, and Justin Timberlake—hit number one on the Billboard 200 chart. For his contributions to the song "Shake Ya Tailfeather," P. Diddy would win his third Grammy.

Such successes aside, Bad Boy had a string of mediocre-selling albums during this period. Several albums struggled to achieve gold

P. Diddy branched out into acting with small roles in films like 2001's Monster's Ball.

SEAN JOHN CLOTHING

After his record label took off, Puffy began to branch out into other business ventures. In 1998, he started his own clothing line, naming it after his real first and middle names. According to the company Web site, Sean John Clothing was intended to "fill a void in the market for well-made, sophisticated fashion forward clothing that also reflects an urban sensibility and style." The clothes focused on males ages 12 to 45, though there were clothes for women and young boys, too.

For Puffy, the creation of his own clothing line was a lifelong dream come true. "I always had the idea that I would start my own apparel line," he said, "but I wanted to make sure the timing was right and that I had the time to devote to it." The clothes were well received by the public as well as in prestigious fashion circles.

(Top) An enormous billboard in New York's Times Square for the Sean John clothing line. (Bottom left) Puffy promotes his clothing line at an event in the Macy's department store in New York.

The Sean John line has since added other merchandise, including cologne, eyewear, and wallets. Today, Sean John products can be found in major department stores across the United States. There are even a few Sean John–only stores in various cities across the country.

The Sean John clothing line has won numerous awards. Today, the company sells more than $500 million each year.

status. Others—including the self-titled debut of the rap duo Loon; *Hot & Wet* from 112; and *One Love*, the comeback album from 1980s singing stars New Edition—failed to sell even 500,000 copies.

OTHER INTERESTS

In 2003, P. Diddy raised $2 million for charity by running in the New York City Marathon. His sponsors for the race included entertainers Jennifer Lopez, Bruce Willis, Ben Affleck, and Oprah Winfrey, as well as New York City mayor Michael Bloomberg. P. Diddy also founded a nonprofit group called Citizen Change, whose goal was to register voters for the 2004 presidential election.

Although his music label may have been suffering from sluggish sales and a dearth of recent hits, P. Diddy found success in other business endeavors. That included his clothing line, Sean John. In 2004, Diddy won the Menswear Designer of the Year award from the Council of Fashion Designers of America. He remained a big celebrity, and soon he would refocus his energies on trying to get Bad Boy back to the top.

5

the dream lives on

By the beginning of 2005, P. Diddy once again began focusing on the music end of his business. And, once again, that meant returning to the Biggie Smalls vault in hopes of jump-starting Bad Boy's record sales. This release, called *Duets: The Final Chapter*, was similar to the Notorious B.I.G. album *Born Again*, which Bad Boy had released six years earlier. Like its predecessor, *Duets* featured leftover studio outtakes Biggie had recorded prior to his death, mixed with raps from other popular artists. They included Eminem, Jay-Z, Snoop Dogg, Mary J. Blige, and, once again, P. Diddy. In less than a year, *Duets* sold more than a million copies, giving Bad Boy another platinum album.

CHANGES

Duets came out just a few months after P. Diddy had sold 50 percent of his Bad Boy record label to industry giant Warner Music. The deal, estimated to be worth about $30 million, gave Warner equal control over all the records Bad Boy had ever produced.

The Bad Boy founder made another personal announcement in August 2005. Once again, he'd decided to change his name. No longer did he want to be called P. Diddy. Now, he just wanted people to call him "Diddy." He unveiled his new Diddy persona at the 2005 MTV Video Music Awards, which he hosted.

Whether it was due to Diddy's name change, Warner's partnership, or a combination of both, Bad Boy enjoyed a couple of hit releases in 2006. June saw the debut of Jasiel "Yung Joc" Robinson, a

Thanks to his many ventures, Diddy has become extremely wealthy. In March 2011, Forbes magazine estimated Combs's total net worth at $475 million, making him the wealthiest figure in hip hop. An August 2011 article in the magazine reported his annual income at $35 million, second only to Jay-Z among hip-hop figures.

rapper from Atlanta. Yung Joc's *New Joc City*, which included the hit single "It's Goin' Down," reached the number-three spot on the Billboard 200 chart.

In August 2006, Bad Boy released the self-titled debut of Danity Kane. The five-member girl group had won the third season of MTV's reality show *Making the Band*. The album *Danity Kane* went to number one on the Billboard 200, en route to selling more than 2 million copies.

===== FAST FACT =====

Yung Joc failed to duplicate the success of his 2006 debut, and his tenure at Bad Boy has been troubled. In 2007, the rapper was arrested when he tried to carry a loaded gun through an airport security checkpoint. That same year, he released his second album, *Hustlenomics*, which was a commercial flop. In 2009, Yung Joc announced his plans to sue Bad Boy for failure to pay royalties and advances.

Later in the year, Diddy released his fourth album, *Press Play*. It included contributions from such artists as Brandy, Christina Aguilera, Nas, Timbaland, and Mary J. Blige. Though *Press Play* debuted at number one on the Billboard 200, sales quickly fizzled. The album struggled to gain gold certification.

DISAPPOINTMENTS

Diddy's dud was part of a string of disappointing releases for Bad Boy. *The Notorious B.I.G—Greatest Hits*, went gold following its March 2007 release. But after that, six straight albums from Bad Boy failed to sell even 500,000 copies.

The dry spell was final broken by Danity Kane's second album, *Welcome to the Doll House*. It was released in March 2008. The album debuted at number one on the Billboard 200, quickly went gold, and was eventually certified platinum.

But *Welcome to the Doll House* wasn't followed by other blockbuster

The all-girl group Danity Kane released two successful albums on the Bad Boy label. The group included (left to right) Wanita "D. Woods" Woodgett, Aundrea Fimbres, Dawn Richard, Aubrey O'Day, and Shannon Bex.

albums. During the remainder of 2008 and through 2009, Bad Boy released a half-dozen commercial flops.

END OF AN ERA?

In September 2009, Diddy signed a deal with Interscope, a label that is part of the huge Universal Music Group and whose roster includes such superstars as 50 Cent, Eminem, and Lady Gaga. According to

Sean Combs has never been married. He has five children. Their names are Justin, Christian, D'Lila, Jessie, and Chance. Here, Diddy poses with the children during the ceremony at which he received a star on the Hollywood Walk of Fame.

the terms of the deal, Warner Music would retain rights to all previous Bad Boy releases, and all artists with Bad Boy at the time of the deal would remain with the Warner-owned label. Interscope would release all future Diddy albums, including *Last Train to Paris*, which was scheduled for release in December 2010. Diddy was also supposed to launch an imprint for Interscope, which, confusingly, would also carry some form of the Bad Boy name.

"With this new deal, I look forward to signing music's next great superstars to the label and continuing the legacy of making great music at my new

FAST FACT

In 2008, Puffy began hosting his own reality TV series on VH1 called *I Want to Work for Diddy*. In the show, contestants battled for the opportunity to become Puffy's personal assistant.

The group Diddy-Dirty Money features Diddy along with singers Kalenna and Dawn Richard (formerly of Danity Kane). The group, shown here at the 2010 American Music Awards ceremony in Los Angeles, has released several hit singles.

home," Diddy declared. "This is the beginning of a new musical era for Bad Boy."

The old era had been marked by many successes. Bad Boy produced 20 platinum albums and sold more than 60 million records worldwide. In the process, the label made Sean Combs rich and famous beyond his wildest dreams. In 2010, according to an August 2011 *Forbes* magazine article, he earned $35 million—second only to Jay-Z in the hip-hop world. Much of Diddy's money came from new business ventures, including ones in the alcohol, television, and film industries. What began as a young man's dream of starting his own record label has since turned into a multimillion-dollar empire.

Chronology

1969   Sean "Puffy" Combs is born on November 4.

1990   Combs is hired as an intern at Uptown Records and drops out of college.

1991   In December, nine people are killed at a charity basketball game organized by Combs.

1993   Combs is fired from Uptown Records and begins Bad Boy Entertainment.

1994   In September, the debut album of Biggie Smalls, *Ready to Die*, is released.

1995   In August, Suge Knight, the president of Death Row Records, ridicules Combs at the Source Hip-Hop Awards. This helps touch off a bitter and bloody feud between East Coast and West Coast rappers.

1996   In September, Death Row rapper Tupac Shakur is murdered.

1997   On March 9, Biggie Smalls is killed in a drive-by shooting in Los Angeles. His second album, *Life After Death*, is released on March 25. Puff Daddy's first album, *No Way Out*, debuts at number one on the Billboard 200 chart when it is released on July 1, thanks in part to the hit single, "I'll Be Missing You."

1999   Combs and two Bad Boy associates are arrested for a December 27 shooting at Club New York.

Chronology

2001 Bad Boy rapper Jamal "Shyne" Barrow is sentenced to 10 years in prison for his role the 1999 shooting at Club New York.

2005 Combs sells 50 percent of Bad Boy Records to Warner Music for an estimated $30 million.

2006 Bad Boy releases *Press Play*, the first album under the Diddy pseudonym (and Combs's fourth studio album overall).

2008 Danity Kane's second album, *Welcome to the Dollhouse*, debuts at number one on the Billboard charts.

2009 Combs signs a deal aligning Bad Boy with Interscope Records.

2010 The Diddy-Dirty Money album *Last Train to Paris* is released in December.

2011 *Forbes* magazine estimates Combs's total net worth at $475 million, making him the wealthiest figure in hip hop.

Glossary

collaboration—an instance in which two or more artists work together on a project.

crossover—the process by which an artist or group popular only with fans of a particular type of music becomes popular with fans of other types of music; an artistic work that achieves popularity outside its original genre.

egotistical—having an exaggerated sense of one's importance; conceited.

entourage—a group of associates who travel with a high-ranking or important person.

entrepreneur—a person who organizes, manages, and finances a business.

explicit—leaving nothing to the imagination; graphic.

genre—a category or type of art.

gold—in the recording industry, a recognition that a song or album has reached the milestone of selling 500,000 copies.

mentor—an older, more experienced, or more powerful person who serves as a guide.

mogul—an important or powerful person in a particular field.

platinum—in the recording industry, a recognition that a song or album has reached the milestone of selling a million copies.

Glossary

posthumous—occurring after a person's death.

protégé—a person who is trained or guided in a particular field by someone with more experience or influence.

reckless endangerment—a legal term used to describe the act of participating in an activity that could result in physical injury or death to another person.

Further Reading

Brown, Jake. *Ready to Die: The Story of Biggie Smalls Notorious B.I.G.* Phoenix, AZ: Colossus Books, 2004.

Evans, Faith, with Aliya S. King. *Keep the Faith: A Memoir.* New York: Grand Central, 2008.

Marcovitz, Hal. *Notorious B.I.G.* Philadelphia: Mason Crest Publishers, 2006.

Ro, Ronin. *Bad Boy: The Influence of Sean "Puffy" Combs on the Music Industry.* New York: Pocket Books, 2001.

Scott, Cathy. *The Murder of Biggie Smalls.* New York: St. Martin's Press, 2000.

Traugh, Susan M. *Sean Combs.* Farmington Hills, MI: Lucent Books, 2010.

Wittmann, Kelly. *Sean "Diddy" Combs.* Philadelphia: Mason Crest Publishers, 2006.

Internet Resources

http://badboyforever.com/

This highly detailed site provides updates on the latest Bad Boy artists and their upcoming releases, as well as a detailed history of the company.

http://www.badboyblog.com/

The latest news on everything related to Bad Boy can be found at this site.

http://rap.about.com/od/hiphop101/a/hiphoptimeline.htm

A detailed timeline of hip-hop, with links to other subjects related to rap.

http://www.diddydirtymoney.com

The Web site of Sean "Diddy" Combs includes new music, videos, tour dates, a blog, and more.

http://www.biggieduets.com/

This site includes information about the life and work of Christopher "Biggie Smalls" Wallace.

Publisher's Note: The Web sites listed on this page were active at the time of publication. The publisher is not responsible for Web sites that have changed their address or discontinued operation since the date of publication. The publisher reviews and updates the Web sites each time the book is reprinted.

Index

Entries in ***bold italic*** refer to captions

JEFF BURLINGAME is an award-winning author of several books, including many dealing with people in the music industry. He and his family reside in Washington state.